THE BOOK OF STUPID LISTS

THE BOOK OF STUPID LISTS

The most ludicrous lists in the world

By Mark Leigh and Mike Lepine

This paperback edition first published in Great Britain in 2006 by

Virgin Books Ltd
Thames Wharf Studios
Rainville Road
London
W6 9HA

First published in Great Britain in 1991 by Virgin Books Ltd

A catalogue record for this book is available from the British Library.

ISBN 10: 0 7535 1114 2
ISBN 13: 978 0 7535 1114 5

The paper used in this book is a natural, recyclable product made from wood
grown in sustainable forests. The manufacturing process conforms to the
regulations of the country of origin.

Typeset by Phoenix Photosetting, Chatham, Kent
Printed and bound in Great Britain by Bookmarque Ltd

Contents

Our Furry Friends

14 Animals with Stupid Names

Ocelot

Gecko

Aardvark

Gnu

Okapi

Aye-aye

Tapir

Dingo

Sperm whale

Cuttlefish

Orang-utan

Ring-tailed lemur

Bandicoot

Caribou

5 Birds' Names That Raise a Snigger

Blue Tit

Coal Tit

Great Tit

Long-tailed Tit

Greater Spotted Arsehole

11 Dogs That Look as Stupid as Their Names Sound

Shar-pei

Pomeranian

Chow-chow

Samoyed

Dachshund

Pug

Chihuahua

Schnauzer

Lasa apso

Shih-tzu

German spitz

5 Stupid Birds That Can't Fly

Ostrich

Penguin

Kiwi

Emu

Dead pigeon

12 Sandwich Fillings for People Who Like the Taste of Insects

Cockroach and cress

Mosquito and egg salad

Weevil and tuna

Flea and coleslaw

Bluebottle and prawns

Bumblebee and tomato

Dung beetle and cheese

Red ant and salmon pate

Dragonfly and Branston pickle

Earwig and coronation chicken

Greenfly and lettuce

Daddy-longlegs and ham on brown bread

10 Pop Stars or Groups Named After Creepy-Crawlies

Adam and the Ants

Ziggy Stardust and the Spiders from Mars

The Beatles

Sting

The Ladybirds

Buddy Holly and the Crickets

Roachford

The Scorpions

Frank Zappa and the Moth-ers of Invention

The Po-lice

12 Stupid Things to Try to Train Your Dog to Do

Handstands

Mechanical engineering

Write its name

Fetch a big bar of chocolate without eating it

Fly a microlite

Fly

Practise safe sex

Say Grace before eating

Climb trees

Complete complex jigsaw puzzles

Play hopscotch with you

Anything he doesn't want to do, basically

10 Stupid Reasons Why the Dinosaurs May Have Died Out

- They contracted 'mad dinosaur disease'
- Prince Philip's ancestors thought it was a 'topping wheeze' to hunt them for sport
- They all became gay
- They didn't watch their cholesterol levels
- They didn't fancy each other
- The Japanese were responsible
- They got hold of a sex instruction manual entitled *Great Sex the Giant Panda Way!*
- They worked too hard, ate too many fatty foods and spent too much time in front of the television set
- They smoked sixty a day
- They lived near a primitive nuclear power station and all the baby dinosaurs got leukaemia

15 Movies with Armadillos in Them

Carry On Armadillo (1964)

Enter the Armadillo (1973)

The Wizard of Armadillo (1939)

Armadillo Day Afternoon (1976)

All the President's Armadillos (1976)

Gentlemen Prefer Armadillos (1953)

A Clockwork Armadillo (1971)

Gone with the Armadillo (1939)

Butch Cassidy and the Sundance Armadillo (1969)

The Silence of the Armadillos (1991)

Armadillo (1976)

Armadillo II (1978)

Armadillo III (1981)

Star Wars: The Phantom Armadillo (1999)

Austin Powers: The Armadillo Who Shagged Me (1999)

16 Things Your Dog Doesn't Understand

- That he's not your superior
- The word 'No!'
- Anything else you tell him in plain English
- Why he shouldn't roll in the mud and then take a nap on your bed
- Why you all suddenly leave the room when he has a wind attack
- That you don't find it absolutely hilarious when, late one night, he suddenly starts staring at an empty corner of the room with teeth bared and hackles raised
- Precisely what's wrong with practising his fiercest, gruffest bark at three in the morning
- That it's not funny to carry your discarded underpants into the room with him in front of guests
- That the furniture is not there for his personal amusement
- Why it's wrong to back Auntie Joan into a corner and guard her

- Why your leg doesn't enjoy it as much as he does
- That other dogs' bottoms are not the most fascinating things in the world
- Why your cat has as much right to sit in the lounge as he has
- Why he should get into the bathtub if he doesn't want to
- Why he shouldn't steal the pate off the table if he can reach it
- Why he shouldn't do exactly what he wants, basically

10 Amazing Books by Thomas Hardy About Fish

The Bream of Casterbridge

Tess of the Herring

Far from the Madding Shoal

Jude the Halibut

The Mullet Major

Desperate Tench

Life's Little Minnows

The Fins of Ethel Sardine

Under the Grey-Green Sea

The Return of the Salmon

...And 10 More by Charles Dickens

A Tale of Two Trout

Haddock and Son

A Christmas Fish

Oliver Tiddler

Nicholas Coelacanth

David Codderfield

The Whitebait Papers

The Old Curiosity Mackerel

Little Coley

Edwin Skate

11 Animals That Are Fat Bastards

The pig

The sea lion

The hippo

The rhinoceros

The elephant

The toad

The sea cow

The walrus

The brontosaurus

The American bison

The whale

8 Different Kinds of Shrew You Couldn't Care Less About

North African elephant shrew

Giant elephant shrew

Masked shrew

Eurasian common shrew

Eurasian water shrew

Northern short-tailed shrew

Bicoloured white-toothed shrew

Sav's pygmy shrew (aka the Etruscan shrew)

11 Creatures Which Sound Rude

The bustard

The great tit

The poodle

The horny toad

The cockatoo

The pronghorn antelope

The winkle

The cockle

The cock

The ass

The sperm whale

The Official Scientific Latin Names for Various Different Types of Dog Poo

- *Squigissimi* (Squidgies)
- *Moccari Admiratio* (Mocha Surprises)
- *Flavi Periculum* (Yellow Perils)
- *Rex Canii Fecii* (King Dog Plops)
- *Dimidium Liquorum Latere* (Semi-Liquid Lurkers)
- *Crispus Turbi* (Curly-Wurlies)
- *Clandestinus Imbuere Cumululi* (Stealthy Tan Clusters)
- *Fulvus Gigasere* (Brown Behemoths)
- *Odor Maximus* (Great Whiffies)
- *Cretosus Putrefacere* (Chalky Crumbles)

Culture Shock

6 Alternative Names for 'Man Friday' if Robinson Crusoe Had Found Him on a Different Day

Man Monday

Man Saturday

Man Thursday

Man Sunday

Man Wednesday

Man Tuesday

10 Stupid Things the Authors of This Book Have Done. (Honest!)

- Dressed up as Arab Sheiks and tried to solicit women from the back of a car

- Stayed up all night looking for flying saucers

- Appeared on national television wearing women's tights, swimming trunks and towels

- Flicked V-signs at passengers out of a first-class railway carriage

- Bunked off school to eat choux buns and read DC comics

- 'Rhinoceros Men from Mars' impressions along Bournemouth Promenade

- Held a children's birthday party in the middle of an A level Government & Politics class

- Made a home video for 'Born To Run', featuring a child's doll and a bottle of Domestos

- Driven to Southend on a whim, simply because it seemed like a good idea at the time

- Agreed that 4 January was a good publication date for their book 'The Naughty 90s' – the one you've *really* never heard of . . .

10 of the Most Embarrassing Publications to Ask for in a Newsagent

- *Reliant Robin World*
- *Aircraft Spotter Monthly* (incorporating *The Virgin*)
- *Premature Ejaculation Sufferer*
- *Coprophilia Weekly*
- *Self-Abuse Gazette*
- *Game-Show Enthusiast*
- *The Vivisectionist*
- *UK Tasty Birds Contact Mag*
- *Pig Fancier*
- *Sunday Sport*

10 Things That Vincent van Gogh Couldn't Do

Count up to two, using his ears

Make full use of a Sony Walkman

Keep more than one paintbrush behind his ears

Wear a pair of sunglasses and keep them straight

Wear a pair of matching stud earrings

Impersonate someone with two ears

Earn the nickname 'Dumbo'

Put his hand on his heart and say that he never once
mutilated his head

Grin from ear to ear

Tell if something was in stereo

10 Stupid Things That Leonardo da Vinci Could Have Been Doing in Order to Make the Mona Lisa Smile

- Opening and closing his flies in time to music
- Doing his impression of Michelangelo pissed
- Telling the one about Pope Julius II, the goat and the lasagne
- Demonstrating a prototype clockwork vibrator that he'd just invented
- Telling her that one day heavier-than-air flight would be possible
- A big wet juicy fart
- Saying that one day this painting would be hanging in the Louvre – which she misheard as 'loo'
- Painting, unaware that he had a big blob of green paint on his chin
- Tickling her nether regions with a long feather duster
- Telling her he was going to pay her ten times more than he actually was

9 Shakespeare Plays That Sound Like Titles of Soft-Porn Videos

Two Gentlemen of Verona

The Merry Wives of Windsor

Antony and Cleopatra

King John

As You Like It

Twelfth Night

Measure for Measure

The Taming of the Shrew

The Rape of Lucrece

12 Unsuitable Performers to Entertain the Frail and Elderly

Eric and his Pyrotechnics Par Excellence

Mr Harwood & his Daredevil Stunt Kittens

Leather Marion's Bondage Half-Hour

The Sudden Loud Noise Experience

DJ Ranking Leroy B's Sound System

The Nudie Royal Lookalikes Show

Sonja the Viper-Juggler and Bill

The Nottingham Slamdancers (audience participation encouraged!)

The Tyrolean Blindfolded Yodelling Tumblers

Billy Jenkins's Horror Roadshow

The Lash Brothers' Whipcrackaway Wild West Show

Danny Tib's Dying Animal Impressions Show

The Number of Buttocks Possessed by 10 Prominent Poets

John Dryden (2)

Andrew Marvell (2)

T.S. Eliot (2)

John Donne (2)

Ted Hughes (2)

Stevie Smith (2)

Arthur Clough (2)

Alfred Lord Tennyson (2)

Robert Frost (2)

William Butler Yeats (2)

Fame and Fortune

12 Nicknames the Elephant Man Had to Endure at School

Floppy Skin

Jumbo Bonce

Repugno

Deformo

Trunky

Snorky Jack

Big Head

Tusker

Nellie

Jumbo John

Pachyderm Features

Norman Lamont

13 Pop Stars with 12 Letters in Their Names

Janet Jackson

Jason Donovan

Chris de Burgh

Stevie Wonder

Kylie Minogue

Johnny Rotten

Cliff Richard

Keith Richard

Art Garfunkel

Roger Daltrey

Mark Knopfler

New Kids On The

Elvis Presley

10 Stupid Things the Waltons Would Never Do

Undermine capitalism

Set fire to their homestead for the insurance money

Indulge in mass incest

Take part in a $60,000 armed bank robbery

Tunnel under Walton's Mountain in search of
valuable uranium deposits

Join the Ku Klux Klan for a laugh

Destroy state property in an orgy of wanton
destruction

Sell their children into bondage

Wear goat masks and worship the devil in a big way

Go to bed with the lights on

6 Greek Philosophers Who Were Also Rappers

L.L. Cool Socrates

Ice T. Plato

M.C. Aristotle

Snoop Pythagoras

Grandmaster Diogenes and his Furious Five

Biggie Pericles

17 Marx Brothers Who Never Made It . . .

(Everyone knows Groucho, Chico and Harpo;
devoted fans will probably have heard of Zeppo and
Gummo, who made rare appearances in Marx
Brothers films – but hardly anyone knows about the
other brothers who never made it into the movies . . .)

Leppo

Homo

Vommo

Flatulo

Sucko

Typhoido

Pricko

Nobbo

Sypho

Pervo

Lino

Fellatio

Incontinento

Thicko

Ringo

Sumo

Crossdressero

10 Stupid Things That John F. Kennedy Might Have Said Just After He Was Shot

Boy! Have I got a migraine!

Ouch!

I think I'm losing my mind

Did you hear that?

Say what?

Oh shit!

Whooo! Good shot!

Anyone know a good brain surgeon?

I need this like a hole in the head

Now I'll never be able to give Teddy those driving lessons

14 Famous People with Rude Names

Urethra Franklin

Epididymis Bosch

Sir Arthur Colon Doyle

J. Arthur Wank

Mark Twat

Jackson Bollock

V.S. Nipple

Edgar Allen Poo

Charles Dickend

Jean-Paul Fartre

Lou Rawls (try saying it out loud)

William Shatner

e.e. cummings

Tony Hancock

The Real Names of Famous Movie Stars

John Wayne (Marion Botty)

Kirk Douglas (Ricky Dibble)

Rudolph Valentino (Harry Sick)

Humphrey Bogart (Dennis Snotrag)

Orson Welles (Prince the Wonder Dog)

Alan Ladd (Ernest Borgnine)

Cary Grant (Archibald Leech)

Ernest Borgnine (Alan Ladd)

Cyd Charisse (Sid Charisse)

Judy Garland (Frances Bumm)

Alec Guinness (Alec Light-Ale)

Marlon Brando (Marlon Stott)

Zsa-Zsa Gabor (Doris Smedley)

Norman Wisdom (Norman Stupid)

Rod Steiger (Sheik Abdullah al Rahmani of Quatar)

Burt Reynolds (Debbie Reynolds)

Anthony Quinn (Pope Gregory XIV)

Joseph Bottoms (Clint Sphincter)

Ginger Rogers (Ginger Buggers)

Once Upon a Time

8 Stupid Pieces of Furniture in King Arthur's Castle, in Addition to His Round Table

Rectangular chair

Square bookcase

Octagonal sideboard

Diamond-shaped cupboard

Hexagonal bed

Elliptical sofa

Triangular bath

Trapezoid wardrobe

The Christian Names of the 6 American Presidents Called 'James'

James

James

James

James

James

James

The Christian name of the 1 American President Called 'Zachary'

Zachary

15 Reasons to Be Glad You Weren't Alive in the 14th Century

- It was utter crap back then
- The Church would burn you alive for having a wart or saying 'Here, kitty, kitty' or being caught in possession of a broom
- The only cure for toothache was to smash your head repeatedly against a wall until it hurt worse than your tooth
- You usually died before you were old enough to vote
- But then, you didn't have the vote anyway
- People with bubonic plague were everywhere, and they put you off your dinner
- You had to dance round a fucking maypole every May
- You spent from dawn until dusk up to your knees in shit
- There was no *Playboy* or *Custom Car* magazine. You had to read the Bible
- But then, you probably couldn't read anyway

- Lepers would come along and breathe on you
- All your orifices officially belonged to the lord of the manor
- By law, you had to practise archery, which is dead boring and hurts the fingers
- Your only entertainment would be watching a field lie fallow
- You wouldn't be alive now to see Keira Knightley

10 Things Viking Berserkers Were Renowned For

Going berserk

Cutting people's heads off

Going purple in the face

Screaming a lot

Spinning in circles with a two-handed battle axe

Thrashing about

Foaming at the mouth

Glazed expressions

Dribbling profusely during combat

Finishing fighting two hours after everybody else

10 Things Viking Berserkers Were Not Renowned For

Baking good cakes

Well-reasoned debate

Charm

Poise

Elegance

Cunning battle plans

Good dress sense

Having a lot upstairs

An active sense of irony

Washing behind their ears

8 Stupid Reasons Why the Romans Built Straight Roads

- To stop the Assyrians opening up corner shops
- The bend had yet to be invented
- Romans had no sense of direction and needed all the help they could get
- They were worried that Celts would smear slippery woad on the corners
- Chariots were not equipped with steering wheels
- They were scared of druids lurking in dark corners
- If they'd had bends, a legion might not see another legion coming the opposite way and collide head on
- Romans were notoriously prone to travel sickness

10 Unlikely Vikings

Wulf the Sensible

Olaf the Interior Decorator

Frank the Berserker

Ethelred Bottom Scratcher

Sedring the Mediocre

Bjorn of Arabia

Horsa the Rather Nice

Tubrg the Ticklish

Kraken the Chubby

Wulfberg the Fresh-Smelling

The Amazing World of Confectionery

9 Stupid Things to Do with a Bar of Chocolate

Throw it in the bin

Unwrap it, smear it with axle grease and then give it to a loved one

Use it as a smear-on deodorant

Eat half, then offer to sell it back to the sweet shop for half the price you bought it for

Smear it all over your face and pretend to be 18 months old

Melt it down and use it as yummy eye shadow

Jump up and down on it, to make your feet look dirtier than they really are

Give the dog a bite before you have one

Attempt to smoke it

Home, Sweet Home

10 Stupid Addresses That you Wouldn't Want to Have

Cheapo Avenue

Condemned Crescent

Syphilis Grove

Wrong Side of Town Drive

Very High Crime Rate Street

Cesspit Place

Site for the Forthcoming Ring Road Lane

Unbelievably High Community Charge Terrace

Cardboard City

Death Row

12 Things That Toddlers Have an Uncanny Ability to Do

- Wake up from a deep, deep sleep just 90 seconds after you finally get to bed

- Cry for one minute longer than you can possibly tolerate

- Poo themselves in a big way, 30 seconds after you've struggled to change their nappy

- Forget to walk, speak or generally act cute as soon as your friends or relatives are watching

- Scream their lungs out as soon as your car gets caught in a stationary motorway traffic jam

- Lose all appetite as soon as you've finished slaving over their favourite dinner

- Hide your keys in a completely different (and equally inaccessible) place each time

- Spurn expensive and impressive toys in favour of a cornflake packet and two yoghurt pots

- Find the only Biro without a cap when your back's turned for 8 seconds

- Always manage to find one of your eyes when playing with a blunt instrument

- Throw up only on clothes that have to be dry cleaned

- Develop mysterious bruises and other marks on their skin 10 minutes before the health visitor comes

20 Stupid Things Your Parents Say to You When You're Young

Don't do that, you'll go blind

Stop picking it, you'll get a hole there

It'll put hairs on your chest

I'll tell you when you're older

Ask your mother

Let the air get to it

Don't leave it, there are starving children in Africa

You treat this house like a hotel

Have you done your homework?

Wait till your father gets home

Don't spend it all at once

Don't rock the chair – you'll loosen the joints

Don't read at the table

Don't play with your food

…Because I say so

You wait until I get you home

Santa won't come if you're not asleep

Have you cleaned your teeth?

Have you cleaned your hands?

Don't say that, dear, it's not nice

11 Stupid Things Children Always Bring Home from School with Them

Crappy balsa wood models that you have to go into raptures about

Infections

Crazes for nasty, overpriced plastic Japanese toys

The F-word

Their lunch boxes, minus the lid

Strange ideas about human reproduction

Invitations to parents' evenings – three months too late

Requests for copious amounts of cash

Scabby, blood-encrusted knees which they want you to kiss better ...

Friends who pick their nose and then cry until they're taken home

Somebody else's gym kit

10 Things You Wouldn't Want to Find on Your Doorstep at Midnight

Your ex-girlfriend, cradling an infant in her arms

A circus clown carrying a carving knife

Two tons of fresh pig manure

A naked Maori with a glazed expression

Four nuns spending a penny and giggling to themselves

A midget with a cutthroat razor

Two midgets with two cutthroat razors

The pilots of the missing Flight 19, each carrying a bouquet of fresh roses

A long-dead relative

A wreath with your name on it

10 Stupid Things to Run up Behind Your Grandad and Yell

BOO!

Die, pig-dog *Englischer* soldier!

Give us all yer cash, old man!

Grandad! Quick! Your buttocks are on fire!

Rhinoceros! Rhinoceros!

Stuka attack! Down, boys! Down!

Grandad! It's the hospital on the phone ... they want
your pacemaker back ...

Grandad! Grandad! Your catheter's leaking!

They've found out! Run for it!

Granny's dead!

12 Stupid Things to Take Into the Bath With You

A plugged-in four-bar electric heater

A school of barracuda

A surfboard

Quick-setting cement

40lb of instant potato mix and a whisk

A speedboat

Four boy scouts and a Polaroid camera

Cat wee-wee scented foam bath lotion

A dead wildebeest

Your water wings

A deep-sea diver's outfit

Your clothes

12 Stupid Things to Say When Your Child Asks 'What Did You Do in the War, Daddy?'

I was a traitor who spied for the enemy

Napalmed an entire village. It was bloody brilliant

Tortured anyone I could get my hands on

Shat myself

Shot myself

Hid under a bed in Canada

Peeled 600,000lbs of potatoes

Went AWOL for two years

Dressed as a woman to avoid conscription

Killed 317 of my own men by accident

Killed 317 of my own men on purpose

Fought for Hitler

11 Stupid Things Children Say When They're in the Back of Your Car

I want to go home

I don't want to go home

Are we nearly there yet?

I want to be sick

I want to go wee-wee

I've just been sick

I've just done a wee-wee

Can I sit in the front?

I'm hungry

I'm thirsty

Wheeeeee! Big jobs!

14 Surnames You Don't Want to Be Born With

Pratt

Shatz

Boggs

Stroker

Widdlecombe

Spunkmeyer

Bottoms

Gay

Crapper

Fish

Wanklin

Tweazlegrunter

Cox

Hitler

10 Stupid and Heartless Things to Put in Your Child's Stocking at Christmas

Nothing

Last year's presents

Last year's presents, all smashed up

A rusty mantrap

The child, head first

The family cat on a skewer

The contents of your wheelie bin

The contents of your bowels

Yourself, disguised as the rampaging, throat-slitting, totally evil bogieman

A note of abuse from Santa

16 Stupid Things to Say When Visiting a Sick Relative

So, how long have you got then?

Need any help with the rectal thermometer?

Breathe on me! Breathe on me!

God, you look like shit!

Can I have first dibs on your jewellery?

Old Mrs Higgins had that. She died

Good morning, I'm the Grim Reaper ...

You smell, I'm going to have to leave now

I thought only sheep caught that ...

Fire! Fire! Everybody out! Quickly!

The will's in the cupboard, is it?

You look forty years older! I didn't recognise you ...

Chemists get prescriptions mixed up all the time, you know

It *starts* as a cold, yes ...

You're hallucinating: I'm not really here

So, just two weeks, eh? What, oh, they hadn't told you ...

8 Stupid Things to Put on Your Answerphone

'I'm here, but I can't be bothered to answer you'

'I'm not remotely interested in what you have to say, so don't bother leaving a message'

A message pretending to be someone else

'Thanks for dialling Leather Fantasy Line. Please leave your name, address and fantasy after the tone . . .

A message in Dutch

'You have dialled the wrong number. Please try again . . .'

The Nepalese national anthem

A four-ton weight

Mind and Body

12 Stupid (But Polite) Ways to Describe Someone Who's Absolutely Obese

Plump

Friendly

Happy

Cuddly

Jolly

Well built

Big boned

A healthy appetite

Chubby

Stout

A nice personality

Quite big

9 Parts of the Body That You Could Quite Easily Do Without

Earlobe

The dangly thing at the back of your throat

Appendix

Little toe

Belly button

Tonsils

Armpit hair

That big spot on your bottom

Nipples (if you're a man)

10 Things You Wouldn't Want to Sit Down on by Accident

The cat

A rusty 4-inch spike

Your dinner

Your last packet of cigarettes

A red-hot poker

A red ants' nest

Your collection of exotic bird eggs

What the cat's just retched up

A complete stranger's hand

A large predatory animal

15 of the Most Embarrassing Things to ask for in a Chemist

Their biggest bottle of super strength acne lotion

Intimate wipes

Pile ointment

Breath freshener

Diarrhoea medicine

Panty shields

Sore nipple cream

Bikini-line strip wax

'Super Jumbo Plus' tampons

Nasal hair trimmers

Douche solution

Flavoured condoms

'Extra Small' condoms

Anything at all to do with warts

Anything at all to do with male virility problems

10 Things That are Bad for You

Anything you enjoy

A bucket of Polish vodka

Throwing yourself into a live volcano

Wayward women

Married men

Radioactive bath towels

Running into a germ warfare plant and inhaling
sharply

Consuming 800 cheeseburgers in 30 minutes

The working week

Death

12 Stupid Examples of Body Language Guaranteed Not to Attract Anyone of the Opposite Sex

- Picking your nose but trying to make it look like you're scratching it
- Picking your nose but trying to make it look like you're squeezing a blackhead
- Getting that annoying bit of earwax out of your ear with a Biro
- Scratching your crotch frantically
- Nodding constantly and smiling inanely
- Trying to touch your left ear with your right hand, over the top of your head
- Sucking your toes
- Breakdancing
- Holding your breath until you pass out
- Going cross-eyed on purpose
- Thrusting your stomach out as far as it will go
- Plunging your finger in and out of your mouth with that knowing look

10 Things You Should Definitely Insist on When You Have a Vasectomy

- Anaesthetic
- Sterilised equipment
- A surgeon who doesn't bear a grudge against you
- A surgeon who's a real surgeon and not some loony in a white coat who wandered into the hospital off the street
- A surgeon who's done this operation before
- Only having the operation you went in for (e.g. not a sex change at the same time)
- A fresh scalpel
- The operating taking place in a proper operating theatre and not on a table in the staff canteen surrounded by half a dozen old cups of coffee and a sticky bun
- A surgeon who doesn't suffer from epilepsy
- Proper neat little stitches, not rivets, staples or a big bulldog clip

Just Plain Stupid

11 Lists You Hate to Compile

- People you owe money to
- All the things that your wife gets in the divorce settlement
- One night stands who might have got you pregnant
- All the words beginning with 'L'
- Reliable character witnesses for your forthcoming trial
- People to apologise to after last night
- Prices, part numbers and dimensions for mind-numbingly dull technical manuals that you have to do as part of your job
- Outstanding bills
- Things to do today
- Things you should've done today
- 11 lists you hate to compile

12 Words You Can Make Rude – Just by Changing One Letter!

Walk

Pits

Ripples

Cant

Bum

Bullocks

Funk

Tip

Skunk

Bus

Dock

Dingpiece

13 Very Dark Colours

Black

Coal Black

Brilliant Black

Pale Black

Light Black

Matt Black

Midnight Black

Peach Black

Royal Black

Noir Grand

Dark Black

Black with a Hint of Black

Navy Black

10 Things That Really Annoy Me About Mark Leigh, by his Wife, Debbie

- He decides he can't find what he's looking for, *before* he even looks

- He decides he doesn't like someone *before* he's even spoken to them

- He always leaves the lid of the biscuit tin just resting on it and not put back firmly

- He slurps drinks

- He insists on putting the toilet roll on the holder *the wrong way round* (i.e. with the loose end nearest the wall)

- The way he sucks peanuts into his mouth (it's so embarrassing)

- He doesn't speak into the mouthpiece when he's on the phone, making him difficult to hear

- He can't blow-dry his own hair properly

- It takes him three attempts to leave the house (unlocking, locking and re-setting the alarm each time) before he decides he *has* got everything he needs

- He made me stop this list at nine things

8 Very Big Numbers

10,548,639

3,359,064,395

26,428,326

996,481,063,491

155,328,749,552

2,179,663,303

100,000,004

43,159,612

10 Words Which We've Printed Upside Down

True

Jacobean

Jollify

Baклava

Invert

Graceless

Ululate

Persona

Rinse

Dynamic

11 Things That Are Greasy

Grease

Fish and chips – if they're done properly

Condoms

Elvis Presley's pillowcase

A Biro that's been dipped in butter

The Uruguayan World Cup squad

A gnu smeared with suntan lotion

That ketchup stain on your best shirt

A heavy metal fan's hair

The cat's bottom in a Thai brothel

Your hair, if you don't wash it for three years

10 Words You Won't Find Anywhere Else in This Book, Except on This Page

Zenith

Downgrade

Aplomb

Tribulation

Gala

Apocryphal

Misadventure

Indiscretion

Incognito

Vociferous

2 Words Written in Morse Code That Look as Though They Might Be Rude But Which, In Fact, Are Not

—.— . .— —.—. .

..—. .— .—. ——

10 Things Which There Aren't Names for

17 Things You Don't Want to Find Yourself in *The Guinness Book of Records* for

Loudest and longest death scream

Person cheated on most often by their spouse

Person cheated on with most partners by their spouse

Person most often referred to as 'that complete dickhead'

Longest recorded time spent on the lavatory by a human being

Most useless person

Highest Council Tax

Highest Council Tax Arrears

Ugliest Human Being of Modern Times

Longest attack of hiccoughs

Most under endowed male

Highest plunge directly on to the face

Longest time spent in an iron lung

Biggest tosser

Most recorded bones broken

Worst dress sense

Longest prison sentence served (unjustly)

10 Things You Wouldn't Want down Your Underpants

A Malaysian bollock-eating lobster

A lump of Number 4 reactor from Chernobyl

A miniature working model of the guillotine bought as a souvenir to celebrate the bicentenary of the French Revolution

The barrel of a sawn-off shotgun which just happens to have a dodgy safety catch

A panicked shark

20 litres of Agent Orange

Your treasured collection of used razor blades, some of which may have only been used for two shaves

A bare copper wire, the other end of which is securely tied to a kite flying in a thunderstorm

A bushel of stinging nettles

Deep skidmarks

10 Stupid Ways to Disguise Yourself Prior to Committing a Criminal Act

- Change your shoes

- Wear your coat inside out

- Smear yourself with boot polish (or whitewash)

- Wear a striped jersey and mask, and carry a sack with 'swag' stencilled on it

- Slash your face with a razor to create a prominent scar

- Cut off an arm so that the police will think a one-armed man committed the crime

- Put on 150lb so that the police will be looking for an obese criminal

- Dress up as the Pope, because no one will suspect the Pope of committing the crime

- Wear a giant penguin suit, so that the police will be convinced the witnesses must be mistaken

- Disguise yourself as *yourself*, so that you can claim you were framed

11 Stupid Ways to Try to Become Totally Ruthless, Undisputed Master of the World

- Ask nicely
- Run for high office in Papua New Guinea
- Find a steady job and hope to work your way up through the ranks to Master of the World
- Try to take over the world when there's nobody looking
- Tell everyone that you're the Master of the World – and hope they'll believe you
- Threaten to have a temper tantrum unless you get world power
- Make a cash offer for it
- Disguise yourself as the Master of the World – and hope everyone falls for it
- Attempt to win the world in a lottery
- Replace all the world's leaders with android doubles who are under your complete control
- Marry the Totally Ruthless, Undisputed Mistress of the World

Love, Sex and Marriage

14 Stupid Things to Put in a Lonely Hearts Ad if You're a Man

Premature ejaculation

Austin Allegro owner

Destitute

Compulsive smoker, drinker and gambler

Transvestite

Insurance salesman

Acne-ridden

Contagious

8 children from a previous marriage

Truly obese

Wife beater

Panties

Pervert

Con artist

13 Things You Don't Want to Hear from the Girl You've Just Taken Home with You

- I have to get up early for work tomorrow

- I suddenly feel very tired

- I like you as a friend

- I can feel my period starting

- I'm a virgin and you'll have to marry me first

- Does this mean we're engaged?

- I feel like talking

- Call it women's intuition, but I know you couldn't hope to satisfy me

- I've changed my mind

- Do me a favour and fuck off

- All that drink you've been plying me with has gone straight to my head. I'm going to be sick.

- Of course the courts cleared me. They said I did it in my sleep, you see . . .

- My last boyfriend had eleven inches. I can't wait to see how you measure up

10 Stupid Ways to Fake Orgasm

- Bash your head repeatedly against the headboard, gasping '*Je t'aime . . . je t'aime . . .*'
- Bounce off all four corners of the room, doing your impression of a steam locomotive
- Say, 'Oh, I've come . .', rather matter-of-factly
- Run out of the room screaming, 'Yesohyesohyesohyes!!'
- Beat your breast and yodel like Tarzan
- Roll off the bed and keep rolling over and over, whispering, '*So good . . . so good . . .*'
- Vibrate violently while conjugating a common Latin verb
- Throw salad cream everywhere and say, 'Well, that's it . . .'
- Grip your partner's sexual organs as tightly as you can, pretending to be lost in the throes of rapture
- Pretend to be unconscious for such an extraordinary length of time that your partner panics and calls an ambulance

2 Stupid Tell-Tale Signs That a Man's a Virgin

He says he is

He says he isn't

10 Stupid Words or Phrases You Wouldn't Want Your Best Man to Use in His Speech

Recent sex-change operation

3-month suspended sentence

Biggest mistake of his life

Syphilis

Gay lover

Biggest slapper in the school

Crap in bed

Virgin

I'd give them three months

Boils

14 Stupid Pet Names for Your Wife or Girlfriend

Whore Slave

Ma Petite Cochon

My Cuddly Warthog

Farty

Dog's Breath

Jumbo Thighs

Dirt Box

Thick Cow

Flatsie

Haemorrhoid Features

Fatso

Vermin Skunk Face

Frankenstein's Ringpiece

Snivelling Toad

The 10 Most Stupid Items to Use to Set the Mood for an Intimate Evening in

- Picture-book of Vietnamese war atrocities
- Bucket of steaming cat entrails underneath a glass-topped coffee table
- Your CD of Stuka dive-bomber sound effects
- Album of press cuttings about your sex-change operation
- Wax effigy of your date with pins stuck in it
- Copy of *American Psycho* with all the good bits underlined and 'Yes!' scrawled in the margins
- Huge pentangle burned into the carpet
- Your spare false leg propped up against the wall, near the door
- Framed photographs of your previous 17 partners
- Framed photographs of your previous 17 big jobs

11 Stupid Things to Say if Your Boyfriend or Husband Catches You in Bed with a Rhinoceros

- Oh God! I thought you were still at the office

- It's not what you think

- I've been meaning to tell you about this for some time

- ... And furthermore, he's Wayne and Cindy's real father!

- I just woke up and there he was

- Darling, you remember my friend Thelma, don't you ...

- Rhinoceros? What rhinoceros?

- Let me tell you, he's ten times the mammal you'll ever be!

- It's a fair cop; he wouldn't fit in the wardrobe

- How do you like my nifty new pyjama case?

- I was feeling a bit horny

10 Stupid Things to Mention When You First Meet the Person of Your Dreams

Your stamp collection

Your 12-month battle against crab infestation

Hard bondage

Albanian socio-political theory

Your 25 yards breaststroke certificate

The tube of Preparation H you always carry with you

Bogies

Your verruca

The somewhat unusual mating habits of the common anteater

That they're the person of your dreams ...

The 10 Most Stupid Things to Say to Your Wife When She Suspects You're Having an Affair with Another Woman

- Hello darling. Guess what, I'm having an affair!

- Goodnight darling, I'm just going off to sleep with my mistress

- Not tonight, darling, I only had it off at lunchtime

- While I'm out, if someone called Sally rings, tell her I'll slip out to meet her as you've gone to sleep

- Slip this basque on. It looked like dynamite on Lisa, so it should be OK on you too ...

- Darling, I've got to fly to Verona on business. Do you know where the condoms are?

- Darling, I'm just going to take the dog out a walk. Have you seen my clean underwear?

- I just thought it was about time I started wearing aftershave again, that's all ...

- Sharon never complains!

- Cop a load of these love bites!

10 Stupid Words and Phrases Used in Pornographic Magazines that *Nobody* Ever Uses in Real Life

Manhood

Porridge gun

Swollen love bud

'Feed me your meat . . .'

Fierce tonguing

Plump love lips

Mound

Up it went for the third time . . .

Nine incher

My luxury apartment

13 Things You Wouldn't Want Your Wife to Take on Honeymoon with Her

Your best man

A chastity belt

A comprehensive listing of when all the ships are due in port

Her lesbian lover

A pair of industrial bolt cutters and a thick leather strap to bite on

Four 15,000-piece jigsaws

A pregnancy testing kit

2-week supply of tampons

Her signed vow of celibacy

The business card of a top divorce lawyer

A monster jar of anti-thrush ointment

Two Turkish musclemen

Her mother

10 Stupid Items of Clothing to Get Your Girlfriend to Dress up in, to Spice up Your Sex Life

Horsehair blanket

Thick argyle sweater and matching mittens

A NASA space suit

The national dress of Greenland

Suit of armour

Anything that makes her look like Judi Dench

Anything that makes her look 4 stone heavier

A brown anorak

A boy scout outfit

Sou'wester and oilskins

10 Stupid (But Apt) Titles for Pornographic Magazines

All-Colour Tosspot!

Sexist Crap!

Inadequates' Monthly

Jerk-Off Pocket Digest!

Mr Masturbator (Pour l'Homme)

Totally Unreal Sex Objects on Parade!

Diddle!

Pocket Billiards International

Sad Lonely Men Only

Stroke!

Heavens Above!

1 Creature That Noah Probably Regretted Putting in His Ark

Woodworm

11 Occasions on Which You Don't Want the Virgin Mary Suddenly to Appear Unto You

- While walking a tightrope over Niagara Falls
- During your psychiatric evaluation
- Just when you're trying to convince your wife that you haven't got another woman in the house
- Just as you're about to bring your jumbo jet in to land at Heathrow
- While indulging in a furtive wank
- Just after you've given the Pope the finger
- Just as you're in the process of applying some Preparation H . . .
- When you're shaving off your pubic hair with a cutthroat razor
- While attempting to summon up the devil
- While dressing up in your wife's clothes and parading up and down in front of the mirror
- While interfering with barnyard fowl

12 Plagues That Moses Could Have Smitten the Egyptians with

- The plague of hair on the palms of your hands so that people look at you funny
- The plague of the first born destined to grow up to become hair dressers and choreographers
- The plague of crocodiles nesting in your girdle
- The plague of being right next door to Libya
- The plague of beautiful maidens who are only interested in your money
- The plague of just missing the chariot to work and having to wait half an hour for the next one to come along
- The plague of running out of eggs just when you *really* fancy an omelette
- The plague of itchy groins in public
- The plague of head colds that just won't go away, no matter how much orange juice you drink
- The plague of hair that you can't do a thing with
- The plague of not being able to get a date on Friday night
- The plague of 40-foot pubic lice

14 Things It Would Be Very Stupid for the Pope to Do

Walk around with a huge black panther straining at the leash

Snigger every time he says, 'You may kiss my ring'

Hit himself on the head with a mallet

Do wheelies on a top-of-the-range Harley

Get someone pregnant

Rip all his clothes off and run shrieking through St Peter's

Record a duet with Madonna

Come out of the closet

Tell everyone it's all been a big hoax ...

Declare that, henceforth, he wishes to be known as 'Lucille'

Drive the Popemobile in a demolition derby

Appear in a Durex commercial

Lose his faith

Use the Turin Shroud to wipe his bottom

Back to School

11 Stupid Things They Teach You in Maths That Mean Bugger All When You Leave School

Logarithms

Matrices

Vectors

Quadratic equations

Long division

Topography

Working out the lowest common denominator

Binary arithmetic

Division of negative numbers

Algebra

How long it would take 3 men to dig 7 holes working at twice the speed

13 Stupid Words or Phrases You Usually Find in Your School Report

Tries hard

Bad influence

Lazy

Heart not in it

Easily distracted

Inattentive

Could do better

Steady progress

Very disruptive

Average

Must concentrate

Sadly lacking

Class comedian

11 Stupid Things You'll Always Find at the Very Bottom of Your Child's Schoolbag

Somebody else's gym shorts

A leaky Biro

A boiled sweet with fluff stuck all over it

One smelly plimsoll

Sandwich crusts

Something black, sticky and totally unidentifiable

A crumpled-up school form you were meant to have
received four months ago

A gaudy pocket calculator with the batteries missing

A broken ruler covered in doodles

The school tie that went missing last term

A joke plastic spider

10 Words You Don't Want to See on Your Child's Report Card

Klepto

Bully

Cretin

Chain smoker

Dense

Failure

Incapable

Despised

Worst

Tasty

7 Stupid Things to Tell Your Children on Their First Day at School

- Teachers should always be referred to as 'Mrs Nobface'

- Bad ghosts live in the school toilets

- If you don't like it, just raise your hand and they'll let you go home

- Spitting at other children will help you make lots of new friends

- I'll come and collect you after an hour

- If you need to go to the toilet, let the teacher know by dropping your trousers

- Lessons don't start until 11 a.m., so there's no hurry to get there, is there?

Science Fictions

9 Smells That Are Quite Unpleasant

A 3-day-old corpse

The underwear of a 3-day-old corpse

The burning exoskeletons of insects heated under a
magnifying glass

A Sumo wrestler's loincloth

A jar of sandwich spread that's been left opened on
top of a warm radiator for 17 weeks

Farts induced by vegetable biryani

The interior of a Japanese whaling ship

The armpit of the person standing next to you on a
crowded train as you're trying to read this book
standing up

Brut 33

10 Plants You Wouldn't Want to Meet in a Dark Alley

Ellison's bushwacking marigold

Rhododendrons hell-bent on revenge

A delinquent foxglove

The Shrub Gang

A carnation that thinks it's a triffid

A lily with a grudge

A psychopathic dandelion

A sweet pea desperate for its next fix of crack

A Venus fly trap with nothing left to lose

A privet hedge with a semi-automatic weapon

10 Unhappy Trees

Weeping willows

Manically depressed palms

Distraught elms

Miserable birch

Inconsolable oaks

Tormented pines

Distressed larches

Suicidal bonsais

Sobbing figs

Peeved firs

10 Stupid Facts About the Sun

It's big

It's yellow

It's quite hot

If you tried to fly there it would take a long time

It gets in your eyes

It doesn't really have a hat on

It's still there, even at night (it's just that we can't see it)

We all revolve around it

If it wasn't there, we'd be cold

Icarus flew too near it (prat)

7 Things That Rutherford Split Before the Atom

His lip

The lip of his arch scientific rival

His head open (after his arch scientific rival smacked him one)

His trousers

His sides (at a stupid joke about relativity)

A banana (inventing a brand-new dessert into the bargain)

His personality

10 Scientists Who Would Have Looked Much Better Without Facial Hair

Louis Pasteur

Alexander Graham Bell

Albert Einstein

Guglielmo Marconi

Galileo Galilei

Thomas Alva Edison

John Logie Baird

Alfred Nobel

Marie Curie

Max Planck

12 Stupid Names to Call Your Racehorse

Lame Boy

Doped Up Git

A Little Slow

Cat-Meat Certainty

Lose Your Shirt

Dunracing Lad

Limpy Sam

Last Past the Post

Rank Outsider

Stewards' Enquiry

Knacker's Choice

Asthmatic Lass

10 Stupid Things to Use as the Baton in a Relay Race

A small cactus

A scorpion

Anything covered in Superglue

Anything white hot

Anything securely manacled to your wrist

A lit stick of dynamite

An anvil

A baton-shaped piece of margarine

Your willie

Someone else's willie

10 Stupid Occupations to Put on Your Passport

Ocelot masturbator

Criminal mastermind

Drugs baron

Professional sperm donor

Locomotive juggler

Self-employed wiggly dancer

Catheter fitter to the crowned heads of Europe

Napalm taster

Unicellular life form

Civil servant

On the Road

10 Stupid Things to Lose on a Train

Your fight against terminal syphilis

All hope of ever finding any survivors

Your way

Your mind

Your struggle against an imperialist society

A case containing all your ticket-forging equipment
with your name and address inside it

Your grip on reality

All sense of direction

Your independence

Face

10 Parts of a Car That Sound a Bit Rude

Wankel engine

Push rod

Half shaft

Sump

Piston

Thrust bearing

Big end

Dipstick

Crank

Ball joint

10 Stupid Ways to Identify a Ferrari Owner

He's got a really small willie

His favourite colour is red

You wouldn't trust him further than you could spit

He thinks Porsches are dull

He's embarrassed when a man asks what car he drives

He's only too willing to admit what car he drives when a woman asks

He tries to act like he's 10 years younger

He tries to act like he's 30lbs lighter

He says things like 'Yeah! Groovy!'

He's got a Ferrari

Wage Slaves

11 Stupid Things for Yes-Men to Say

I don't think so

Perhaps

Never!

No

No siree

Maybe

Negative

I'm not sure

Let me think about it

Definitely not

Not for a million pounds

12 Stupid Jobs Guaranteed Not to Impress Your Girlfriend's Parents

Professional drag artiste

Chief vivisectionist

Serial killer

Staff training officer at Woolworth's

Mortician

Anarchist

Commander of a Japanese whaling fleet

The man who cuts the electricity off in old people's houses

Sperm donor

Gigolo

The man who centrifuges urine down at the local hospital

Senior Vice President of Al Qaeda

4 Cruel and Stupid Things to Do at Someone's Leaving Party

- Spike the office coffee machine with laxative before the party, so that no one turns up and she thinks everyone hates her

- Wrap up the coffee machine and present it to her, saying, 'We won't need this to keep us awake now you're going'

- Say, 'I tried to organise a collection for you but, strangely, no one seemed to have any money on them all week, so I made you this necklace out of paperclips and a hat out of A3 cartridge ... I hope you'll think of us whenever you wear them'

- Don't bother to get the card signed – just staple the internal office telephone list to it

10 Things Which Will Not Help Your Career Prospects

Chronic BO

Slaughtering your company's best customers in a Satanic death ritual

Headbutting the chairman

Dressing up as a saucy French maid at the annual sales conference

Appearing on the telly to complain about your company's lousy products

Using kung fu on junior staff

Being caught taking the personnel manager's wife over the office photocopier

Crapping in the fax machine and then repeatedly trying to fax it through to your Glasgow office until forcibly restrained by Security

Pretending that you suddenly speak only Flemish

Getting a degree

11 Jobs It's Unrealistic to Expect You'll Ever Have

US Navy 'Top Gun' fighter pilot

Prime minister of Belgium

Product tester for Budweiser

Spiritual leader of the Cheyenne Indians

Mel Gibson's double

Captain of the Starship *Enterprise*

Special adviser to the United Nations on confectionery matters

A hitman for Millets

Kim Basinger's body slave

Melvyn Bragg's martial arts instructor

Anything that's much good, well paid or satisfying

10 Annoying Things About Stupid Photocopiers

- They switch to A3 as soon as you start to copy something that's A4

- They switch to A4 as soon as you start to copy something that's A3

- They're never switched on when you get to work especially early

- They always jam just when you're photocopying something personal, like the manuscript for a book

- The 'low paper' warning light comes on for no apparent reason

- 1 page out of every 20 that you put through on automatic feed does not get copied

- Whenever the paper runs out, the nearest ream is two floors away

- A queue immediately forms just as soon as you think the coast is clear and you can copy your CV

- There's always one staple you forget to remove that jams up the automatic feed

- The repair man always chats up the one secretary you're trying to get off with

1 Stupid Thing That People Who Work in Advertising Should Never Tell Clients

The truth

10 Stupid Signs to Put in Your Shop Window if You're Having a Sale

We're not having a sale!

Closed!

Everything mustn't go!

!ELAS

Only crap left

Everything twice the price!

First few days!

Everything must stay!

Massive increases!

Armadillo!

10 Stupid Questions to Ask at Your Job Interview

Who's that old bag in the photo on your desk?

How much money do you keep in the safe overnight?

When was the last time you had a bath?

My mate works here. He says it's money for old rope.
Is that right?

How much sick leave can I take before questions get
asked?

What is the capital of Mozambique?

Do you 'go'?

Is that a wig?

Is that all you're paying, you tight-fisted git?

Do you mind if I roll a joint? I can't get through the
day without one

3 Particularly Stupid Ways to Try and Make Friends at the Office

Hold a 'Who is the Real Father of the Receptionist's Baby' Sweepstake:

Jim the Janitor 70-1

Dean in Despatch 3-2

Mr Jones, Company Accountant 500-1

Richard in Sales 7-1

Bob in Sales 6-2

Larry in Sales 5-1

Jonathan in Sales 2-1

One of the decorators 5-2

The man who services the photocopier 11-2

Mr Papadopolous from the sandwich bar 20-1

Her driving instructor 8-1

Her boyfriend, Les 9,000-1

Write a crossword for the in-house magazine

Across

1. Sleeps with customers to obtain orders (5,5)

4. Jon in Accounts's big secret. He's – (3)

7. The typing pool reckon his is the smallest (4,6)

9 . Lisa's just a girl who can't say – (2)

11. Liz is only going out with him for his money (3,5)

12. Cross-dresser in Marketing (first name) (4)

15. Rachel lost this at 12 (9)

16. Who we hide from when we go down the pub (6,6)

18. Tnuc – anagram of what Brian calls the MD (4)

20. What Rick Harris has apparently been one short of since Korea (4)

22. Smells (surname) (9)

23. Michelle in Bought Ledger's favourite sex act (initials) (2)

25. Is for the chop, but doesn't know it yet (first name) (5)

28. The fattest girl in the company (5,7)

30. Says she's a natural blonde (4,5)

31. Must spend all of £25 on his suits (4,7)

Down

1. Didn't get kissed under the mistletoe at the last office party (because he's repulsive) (3,8)

2. Receives backhanders from the photocopier suppliers (surname) (8)

3. Boyfriend just left her for her younger sister (first name) (5)

4. Gave Katy in Personnel gonorrhoea (6,4)

5. Has vaginal warts according to 1 across (4,7)

6. Caught masturbating in stock room and claimed to have knocked over the Tipp-Ex (3,8)

8. Has permanent PMT, according to the typing pool (surname) (6)

10. Naffest haircut in western world (surname) (9)

11. Secretly phones her boyfriend in Australia at 11 every day (surname) (8)

12. Failed miserably to get off with 23 across on office outing (4,7)

13. Has a crush on the MD (surname) (3)

14. What Phil and Shelley do on overtime (slang) (4)

15. Our nickname for Julie (slang) (4)

17. He's using Valerie – and she's too young to see it (6,4)

19. So desperate, she's turned to a dating agency (surname) (7)

21. Says the MD's secretary looks like an iguana (4,5)

22. Urinated in the supervisor's coffee mug for a dare (first name) (4)

24. Petty cash forms are a major work of fiction (surname) (6)

25. Two-timing Paul in Goods-Inwards with 4 down (first name) (2)

26. Hasn't lost it yet – and he's 28 (first name) (3)

27. Feeds half his work into the shredder when no one's looking (surname) (3)

29. Makes such loud noises in the Ladies that we can hear her in reception (first name) (3)

Get hold of someone's ledger – and change all the 5s to 8s

12 Phrases You Don't Want to Overhear When Your Doctor's Talking About You

2 months maximum

2 inches minimum

I'd say 50-50, if that

Who knows?

Who cares?

Below the knee

Below the neck

Big strap to bite on

Impotent for the rest of his life

Next of kin

Isolation ward, and hurry!

Call the circus

5 Stupid Things Mark Wishes He Could Do at Work

Have a helper monkey on roller skates that wore a fez and a red waistcoat

Incentivise staff to work faster by means of a baseball bat with a nail through it

Exert mind control over his clients to make them submissive and whimper like whipped dogs in his presence

Order selected girls to wear swimwear in the office

Take home an extra £25,000

10 Jobs You Don't Often See Advertised Down at Your Local Careers Office

Nazi hunter

Speaker of the House of Commons

Atomic physicist

Double agent

Ranch hand

Space shuttle pilot

Human guinea pig

Pioneering brain surgeon

Queen

Film director

11 Stupid Jobs Guaranteed Not to Impress Your Boyfriend's Parents

Dominatrix

Surrogate mother

Vibrator tester

Traffic warden

Gangster's moll

Sexologist

Masseuse

Trollop

Saucy kissogram

Professional mistress

Female impersonator

What a Wonderful World

8 Rivals to the Infamous 'Bermuda Triangle'

The Bahamas Oblong

The Montserrat Trapezium

The St Lucia Circle

The Jamaica Ellipse

The Barbados Rhomboid

The Trinidad and Tobago Parallelogram

The Antigua Hexagon

The Kennington Oval

5 Countries with Flags That Are Quite Difficult to Draw

- Bhutan (rectangle divided into red and orange triangles with some kind of ornate Chinese-looking serpent in the middle)

- Dominica (something that looks like a green parrot in a red circle, surrounded by ten green stars. The circle is in the centre of a yellow, black and white striped cross with green bits in the corners)

- South Korea (a ball made up of interlocking 'squiggly' red and blue shapes on a white background. Around the ball are four different patterns that look as though they're from a 'Spot the Odd One Out' test)

- Papua, New Guinea (rectangle divided into two triangles. The black one contains six white stars, four big ones and two smaller ones, while the red triangle contains some sort of tropical bird with a long tail)

- Brazil (yellow diamond shape set in a green rectangle. In the yellow diamond is a sort of blue globe with a band running where the equator should be. There's some writing or symbols in this band but the picture in the reference book we're using is too small to make it out properly)

11 Stupid Things to Tell Foreign Tourists in London

- It's considered good luck to stroke a guardsman's busby
- The nearest tube station to Buckingham Palace is Ongar
- You can fish for salmon off Westminster Bridge
- Horatio Nelson was the founder of London and had four pet lions
- It is almost obligatory to haggle with taxi drivers over the fare
- The traditional term of address for a London policeman is 'wanker'
- A yellow line indicates free parking for one hour (a double yellow line indicates two hours)
- There is no speed limit along the Embankment between 11 p.m. and 5 a.m.
- All Commonwealth citizens are entitled to one private audience with the Queen each year. Simply present yourself at the main gate in formal dress
- The Old Kent Road is famed for its gay pubs
- In summer, nude bathing is permitted in only one of the Royal Parks; this is St James's Park, off the Mall

91 *Real* Places in America Which Sound Stupid

Arab, Alabama

Avon, Alabama

Bibb, Alabama

Coy, Alabama

Lower Peach Tree, Alabama

Moody, Alabama

Opp, Alabama

Pisgah, Alabama

Prattville, Alabama

Snead, Alabama

Wetumpka, Alabama

King Salmon, Alaska

Bagdad, Arizona

Chloride, Arizona

El Mirage, Arizona

Tuba City, Arizona

Winkelman, Arizona

Biggers, Arkansas

Flippin, Arkansas

Grubbs, Arkansas

Tontitown, Arkansas

Weiner, Arkansas

Loleta, California

Lompoc, California

Pismo Beach, California

Truckee, California

Weimar, California

Dinosaur, Colorado

Hygiene, Colorado

Security, Color ado

Swink, Colorado

Orange , Connecticut

The Norman G. Wilder Wildlife Area, Delaware

Cocoa, Florida

Homosassa, Florida

Ponce de Leon, Florida

Bibb City, Georgia

Chickamunga , Georgia

Experiment, Georgia

Montezuma, Georgia

Social Circle, Georgia

Zebulon, Georgia

Fruitland, Idaho

Idaho, Idaho

Energy, Illinois

Kankakee, Illinois

Odin, Illinois

Vermillion, Illinois

Munster, Indiana

Poseyville, Indiana

Santa Claus, Indiana

Tippecanoe, Indiana

Early, Iowa

Lost Nation, Iowa

Mechanicsville, Iowa

Titonka, Iowa

Pratt, Iowa

Tonganoxie, Iowa

Big Clifty, Kentucky

Cranks, Kentucky

Flat Lick, Kentucky

Raccoon, Kentucky

Zebulon, Kentucky

Truth or Consequences, New Mexico

Grosse Tete, Louisiana

West Peru, Maine

Princess Anne, Maryland

Whiskey Bottom, Maryland

Dorothy Pond, Massachusetts

North Uxbridge, Massachusetts

West Acton, Massachusetts

Ovid, Michigan

Vulcan, Michigan

Knob Noster, Missouri

Pilot Knob, Missouri

Flathead, Montana

Cheesequake, New Jersey

Dickey, North Dakota

Gackle, North Dakota

Dry Run, Ohio

Mingo Junction, Ohio

Cement, Oklahoma

Talent, Oregon

Berks, Pennsylvania

Wounded Knee, South Dakota

Soddy-Daisy, Tennessee

Deaf Smith, Texas

Lolita, Texas

Bland, Virginia

Isle of Wight, Virginia

Belgium, Wisconsin

The 2 Things That Are Fundamentally Wrong with Belgium as a Nation

It exists

Belgians live there

10 Unsuitable Names for Brutal Fascist Dictators

Fred

Bobby

Chuck

Benny

Elvis

Nobby

Franky

Tim

Bert

Ian

36 *Real* Places in America Which Sound Rude

Boggstown, Indiana

Hornell, New York

Beaver, Kentucky

Trussville, Alabama

Prattville, Alabama

Fruitdale, Alabama

Bald Knob, Arkansas

Bent, Colorado

Grays Knob, Kentucky

French Lick, Indiana

Floyds Knob, Indiana

Lolita, Texas

Rogersville, Kentucky

Flushing, Ohio

Sodus, New York

Cockeysville, Maryland

Colon, Michigan

Big Beaver, Pennsylvania

Climax, Michigan

Licking, Missouri

Big Horn, Wyoming

Pollock, Idaho

Coxsackie, New York

The Little Big Horn, Montana

Butte Valley, Nevada

Hooker, Nebraska

Biggers, Missouri

Cokato, Minnesota

Butte City, California

Crested Butte, Colorado

Willimantic, Connecticut

Tampa, Florida

Peoria, Illinois

Effingham, Illinois

Intercourse, Pennsylvania

Wanker's Corner, Oregon

The Top 10 Causes of Death in Belgium

- Boredom
- Falling off bicycles
- The stress of playing Belgian Trivial Pursuit
- Shock induced by something interesting suddenly happening
- Suicide after being refused an emigration permit
- Accidental exposure to a fairly interesting paperback or magazine
- Falling into a coma and having Belgian doctors try to revive you by playing you a personal message from Belgium's top pop star
- Overdosing on chocolate truffles
- Exhaustion brought about by trying to find something interesting to do on Saturday night
- Simply losing the will to live

7 Things the Japanese Kill Which They Shouldn't

Whales

Dolphins

Porpoises

Anything else that is endangered

The Western electronics industry

Any concept of fair trading practices

POWs

11 Things It Must Be Very Easy to Sell to the Japanese

Elevator shoes

Plastic yellow dick extensions

Penis enlargers

Dental braces

Harpoons

Blue whale ashtrays

Anything else that was once an integral part of an endangered species

A self-help book entitled *How to Work Harder and Die Younger*

A matching set of dolphin-skin luggage

Anything their company says they should have

The idea that they can totally ignore what the rest of the world thinks

11 Things That the Belgians Are Not Very Good at

Throwing wild parties

Letting their hair down

Pop music

Holding their drink

Telling dirty jokes

Starting trends

Vandalism

Football hooliganism

Revolutionising the way we live

Making major motion pictures

Celebrating (but, to be fair, they have never had anything to celebrate)

11 Things That the Belgians *Are* Good at

Staying at home with a good book

Listening to the wireless

Keeping the garden and allotment in good order

Making luxurious confectionery

Knitting and fretwork

Wearing sensible sweaters and comfortable shoes

Knowing when they need a haircut

Remembering people's birthdays

Keeping neat scrapbooks of recipes and do-it-yourself tips

Washing their cars at the weekend

Masturbating

8 Unofficial Black Market Currencies of Turkey

Bribes

Black-market US dollars

Pretty young boys

Opiates

Squat-thrusts

Lambs sold into wool slavery

Second-hand copies of *All-Naked Bashi Bazouks*

Reach-arounds

Day by Day

10 Stupid New Year's Resolutions

Take up smoking

Try and halve your salary

Put on 84lbs

Breathe only once every 40 seconds

Assassinate a foreign dignitary

Put chocolate biscuits down your underwear every
day for the whole year

Sell your new car for £3.50

Spend less time with your family

Learn to recite the Koran in fluent Turkish

Take this stupid book back to the shop

10 Stupid Advantages of Being 3 Feet Tall

- You can save money by wearing children's clothes (but then again, who wants to go through life wearing sailor outfits or blue velvet pinafore dresses with lace collars?)

- If a bullet was coming towards you 4 feet off the ground, it would miss you easily

- You're twice as tall as someone who's only 1' 6" tall

- You're a veritable giant amongst men compared with people who are only 1" tall

- You can headbutt bullies in the nuts

- You can look through keyholes without stooping

- You can get your identical twin to stand on your shoulders, cover yourselves with a long coat and get into an '18' film

- If you're destitute you need only a small cardboard box to live in

- If you're writing a dissertation on 'The Smell of People's Crotches', you're perfectly placed to do your research

- You're virtually guaranteed a part in *Snow White II: The Adventure Continues*

The 10 Least Popular Wallpaper Designs

High-velocity bullet exit wound

Fly on a windscreen

Ruptured spleen

Dead cat by the roadside

Benito Mussolini's bottom

Steaming turd

Interlocking swastikas

Burning orphans

TV interference

Red flock

10 Clues That Your Flatmate Might Be a Serial Killer

- He leaves the flat every night at 11 p.m. with an axe and comes back in the early hours of the morning, saying that he's 'been for a breath of fresh air'

- He's forever asking to borrow your blood Stain Devil

- He's always looking through the phone book and writing down names and addresses completely at random

- He changes his name by deed poll to 'Hannibal'

- He looks longingly at the skinned carcasses hanging in the butcher's window – even though he's a vegetarian

- He's always receiving brochures from surgical supply companies in the post

- His Black and Decker workmate is covered in what he claims is 'red paint'

- The scarf he wears looks suspiciously like a small intestine

- There's a naked leg sticking out from under his bed

- He's forever dragging things to the wheelie bin at the back of the flats in the dead of night

9 Stupid Things You'll Always Find in a Public Toilet

- A strategically placed spyhole through to the next cubicle
- Pervy and disgusting graffiti on the inside of the door that you feel compelled to read, even though you're repulsed
- A lone turd, floating
- Cheap toilet paper that's either abrasive or greasy
- Cigarette burns on the edge of the seat or on the top of the hot air dryers
- An unidentified substance on the handle that you discover by accident only when you come to flush
- A lock that doesn't
- A puddle of a strange, yet familiar-smelling liquid on the tiles
- Roller towels designed so that 78 people use the same 2-foot length of linen

10 Stupid Things You Won't Find in a Typical Amish Household

A multiplay CD system and the whole set of Iron Maiden albums

A huge poster of Freddy Krueger

An Uzi

Cocaine with a street value of $600,000

The keys to a supercharged Pontiac Trans Am

27 back issues of *Playboy*, some with 'water damage'

A wardrobe full of bright, skimpy beachwear

A fridge crammed full of Buds

Edible underwear

A bottle of strawberry-flavoured 'Joy-Jelly'

16 Stupid Things That Secretaries Constantly Talk About

Their boyfriend, Dave

Anyone else called Dave

Their ex-boyfriend

Dave's ex-girlfriend

Their hair

Their clothes

Dave's hair

Dave's clothes

Getting another job

Mel Gibson

Going to some club

Going on holiday

Their best friend

Their best friend's hair

Dave's job

Any combination of any of the above

15 Stupid Things We Bet You've Always Wanted to Do

Walk up a 'down' escalator

Drive your car on purpose into the asshole who just cut you up

Grope the person next to you on a crowded train

Carry a big gun

Answer a lonely hearts ad

Hide in a department store and then wander around it alone after closing time

Pose for a nudie mag

Shoplift

Kick a skinhead in the bollocks

Join the mile-high club

Photocopy your bottom

Measure your willie

Have an affair

Ask Ulrika Johnsson for her autograph

Tell the boss just what a wanker he really is

10 Stupid Things That Prove You're 'Well 'ard'

- Floss with barbed wire
- Drink 5 raw eggs and a bottle of Johnny Walker before breakfast
- Sing 'Sweet Child of Mine' at the top of your voice in the reference library
- Do a poo without washing your hands afterwards
- Do a poo without taking your trousers down beforehand
- At your wedding, when the vicar says 'Does anyone present object?', say, 'Yes, me' and then go home
- Wet shave with your eyes closed
- Punch a copper in the head for no apparent reason
- Punch yourself in the head for no apparent reason
- Yell, 'Whoo! Right through the head!' when Bambi's mother gets shot

What Your Best Friend Says
(and What She Really Means)

- 'That look is really you.' (Cheap, uncoordinated and trashy)

- 'Of course it suits you.' (You always look that rough)

- 'I won't tell a soul, cross my heart.' (Where's my telephone book?)

- 'Of course it's not too small.' (You're just too large)

- 'Of course it's not too revealing.' (I can't wait to see their faces!)

- 'I wouldn't be telling you this if I weren't your friend.' (And didn't enjoy stirring it)

- 'Perhaps I shouldn't be telling you this …' (I can't wait to tell you this!)

- 'Maybe marriage will change him …' (I give the two of you six months, tops)

- 'No one will ever guess.' (Until I tell them, that is)

- 'You look fabulous!' (Tarty cow …)

- 'It's just what I've always wanted!' (You wait until your birthday …)

- 'Will you take a friendly word of advice . . .' (Or 20 minutes of calculated, vitriolic, malicious, catty criticism masquerading as advice?)

- 'Why don't you give him another chance?' (The last time was soooooo funny)

- 'You look like the perfect couple . . .' (Laurel and Hardy)

- 'Goodness knows what it must have cost you!' (£12.99 including VAT – which is half what I spent on you, you cow!)

- 'I just don't know how he found out.' (Unless me telling him had anything to do with it)

- 'I love those jeans on you.' (Because they accentuate your child-bearing hips)

- 'Everybody goes through it.' (If they're chronically plain and dull, that is . . .)

- 'That's the perfect dress for you!' (I can't be bothered to go back to all the other shops)

12 Unsuitable Topics of Conversation at a Dinner Party

Rigor mortis

Enemas

The dog's boil

Your boil

Ethiopia

Where that stuff between your toes comes from

How ugly the hostess is

The art of Sam Peckinpah

Where exactly the *vas deferens* is to be found

Your strange habit of spitting in any food you cook

Glass eyes

The high local incidence of burglary when couples go
out to dinner parties

28 Things You've Probably Got in Your Handbag Right This Very Minute

- A crumpled Danielle Steel paperback

- Some loose change

- Lipstick

- Make-up mirror

- A quarter of a packet of stale Polos

- A disposable lighter (empty)

- Hairspray

- A crumpled-up clipping from a problem page

- A crumpled-up, used Kleenex . . . smeared with make-up

- A crumpled photo of your boyfriend

- A crumpled photo of your parents

- A powder compact

- A book of matches from a restaurant

- A phone number you jotted down, but can't remember whose

- A huge bunch of keys on a stupid novelty key ring

- Two unpaid bills

- Half an old chocolate bar covered with fluff
- Credit-card counterfoils
- The cap from an eyeliner pencil
- A nail file
- 1 stick of Juicy Fruit
- 3 loose tampons
- A dirty hairbrush
- Assorted receipts
- A purse
- A torn-out recipe you'll never make
- A diary you hardly ever use
- An old tangerine peel squashed down into one corner

8 Stupid Things to Do in the Clothes Shop

- Put all the size 10 dresses on size 14 hangers

- Ask the shop assistant if you can have a dress like hers, only two sizes smaller

- Wait until someone picks up a dress and heads for the changing room. Pick up an identical dress in the smallest size available and then follow her in. While she's undressing, swop the dresses over

- If someone asks you to do them up at the back, pretend to be violently struggling. Dig your knee into the small of her back and tug at the zip, puffing and panting. Say, 'I'll have to go and get a shoe horn' – and leave

- Ask the shop assistant for a dress like hers, only one that fits properly

- Find the most revolting dress in the entire shop and start enthusing about how trendy and exciting it is. Wait until the stampede for it starts and then slip out of the shop

- While someone is busy trying on a swimsuit, pick up all her discarded clothing, walk out, hand it to the assistant and say, 'No thanks. You can put them back now'

- When someone asks you to help them on with a dress, run a Stanley knife down the seam. Tell her to cross her arms to make sure it fits

18 Stupid and Heartless Things to Say in a Communal Changing Room

- That's a bit expensive just for a dare, isn't it?

- Excuse me, but have you seen the back of your knicks?

- I saw a dress just like that one in Woolworth's yesterday

- Hey! Get out of here, you filthy pervert! Oh, I'm sorry. I thought you were a man ...

- I had a dress like that. My boyfriend made me throw it away because he said it made me look like Edna Everage

- Pardon me, but I think that will clash terribly with your spots ...

- Excuse me, but would you stop staring at me? Yes, *you*

- Look, if you're that desperate to attract a man I'll fix you up myself

- Excuse me for asking, but you seem to know something I don't. Is the 'plain, severe and drab' look in this season?

- I'd get some acne cream to go with that backless dress if I were you

- Size 12? That's a bit optimistic, isn't it?

- Hi, I'm from Weightwatchers

- I wouldn't buy that dress if I were you. All it does is accentuate your roots

- God. You'll have to shave those legs if you want to wear that ...

- Excuse me, but since you're obviously colour blind would you like any help?

- Isn't it funny how some clothes just accentutate the tummy like that?

- God, you're fat. Don't you care about yourself?

- I'm sorry. I owe you an apology. I'm the store detective. I followed you in here because I thought you'd stuffed six dresses, four skirts and a raincoat up your jumper, but I can see now that it's really all you ...

10 Things You *Really* Don't Want to See First Thing in the Morning

- That half-drained bottle of whisky from the night before
- The alarm clock telling you it's 10.30
- Yourself in the mirror
- Dried spew in your partner's hair (which you know you'll have to tell them about ...)
- The washing-up you left in the sink, in the hope that it would somehow do itself
- A big rip in the condom you dumped on the bedside cabinet
- The remains of the Chinese takeaway all over the coffee table
- Bonnie Langford plugging something on Breakfast TV
- Yesterday's contraceptive pill, next to the glass of water ...
- What the dog did in the night ...

10 Charities You'd Have to Be Stupid to Make Donations to

Save the Cockroach

The Shoot the Elderly Campaign

The Distressed Nazi Gentlefolk Association

The Duchess of York's Appeal for better skiing
conditions in Klosters

The Help the Rich and Privileged Campaign

Famine Relief for Switzerland

Shotgun Aid (helping to keep blood sports
enthusiasts armed and ready!)

Sponsored Giant Panda-Eating

The Donate Your Kidneys to Rich Arabs in Harley
Street Clinics Appeal

The Moonies